# *Sir Gawain And Other Stories*

# *Sir Gawain And Other Stories*

## Myths And Legends Retold Collection

### Avril Sabine

*Cracked Acorn*

*Productions*
*Australia*

Sir Gawain And Other Stories

Myths And Legends Retold Collection

Published by

Cracked Acorn Productions

PO Box 1365

Gympie, Queensland 4570

Australia

978-1-925941-35-7 (Kindle)

978-1-925941-36-4 (EPUB)

978-1-925617-06-1 (Large Print)

Genre: Myths and Legends Retold Short Story




Cover design by Caitlyn Petersen

# Books

Sir Gawain And The Maid With The
Narrow Sleeves

*

Princess Ilse, The Giant's
Daughter

*

Ion, Son Of Apollo

# Sir Gawain
# And The
# Maid With
# The Narrow
# Sleeves

During his journey, Sir Gawain is unable to join a tourney due to more pressing matters. Falsely accused, he's defended by a young girl sorely in need of help. As a knight he's sworn to protect the defenceless, but doing so could jeopardise his own affairs.

*

People have been telling stories since the beginning of time. Fairytales, folklore, myths and legends are among some of the stories that have been told over and over through the centuries. The basic story remains the same, but each storyteller adds their own style, sometimes adding something unique to the tale.

*

This story was written by an Australian author using Australian spelling.

# Chapter One: Gawain

On his way to Cavalon, Sir Gawain came across a troop of knights followed by a squire on foot, leading a Spanish charger. Around the neck of the horse hung a shield. It was one he didn't recognise. Fearing he might be riding towards trouble, Gawain rode up to the squire. Slowing the pace of both the horse he rode and the one he led, to match that of the squire, he nodded towards the troop that had ridden by. "Tell me, whose troop is that?"

"Sir, it's the troop of Meliance of Lis, a brave knight."

"Is he your knight?"

The squire shook his head. "No, Sir. My master is Teudaves. A knight equally as worthy."

"I know Teudaves," Gawain said. "Where is he? "

"He's gone ahead to a tourney, Sir. Meliance of Lis has undertaken a tourney against Thiebault of Tintagel. You should join Thiebault's side, Sir."

He stared at the squire for a moment. Maybe the lad was mistaken. "Didn't Thiebault raise Meliance of Lis in his own home after the lad's father died?"

"Aye, Sir. On his deathbed, Meliance's father asked Thiebault to take care of his son. Thiebault cherished and protected the lad until

Meliance fell in love with Thiebault's oldest daughter, Claudine. Mind you, it wasn't Thiebault who objected to the match. The lass told Meliance she could only love a knight, so he set off to become one. When he returned a knight, he asked her if she could now love him. She told him no."

"Is that why there's a tourney? Meliance is upset at being rejected?" Gawain wouldn't have thought so considering all he'd heard of the young man. It seemed out of character.

"No, nothing like that. Claudine told him she could never love someone who hadn't achieved great feats of arms in her presence so she could see how much effort he was willing to expend to earn her love."

Gawain looked in the direction the troop was heading. "He must love her very much. One can only hope that this time she'll be happy with his efforts."

"Will you join the tourney, Sir? The castle needs every knight with how determined Meliance is to prove his love. Or do you have other matters to attend to?"

"That is my affair." He didn't want to explain the reason for his journey. Not unless it was necessary. Thinking he might have spoken too harshly, he added, "Thank you, lad. And a good day to you." With a nod, he urged his horse forward, the one he was leading following along. It was no one's business but his own why he needed to travel to Cavalon. He forced away the anger that always filled him at the thought of needing to go there. Instead he focused on Meliance and his lady. The knight must love her greatly to go to so much trouble.

Gawain rode towards Tintagel, having no choice but to pass through the town since it was on the way to Cavalon. When he arrived, he found the gates had been walled up with stones and mortar and a guard stood in front of them.

"What is wrong?" Gawain asked.

"It's the council, Sir. They're afraid the tourney will cause the castle to be ruined and aren't allowing it to go ahead."

"Is there no way to get inside?"

The guard gestured further along the wall. "There's a small gate that might still be open, Sir."

With a nod in thanks, Gawain rode to the next gate. Reaching it, he found it closed and locked and decided to rest his horses in a field below a tower. Dismounting under an oak, he hung up his shields and unsaddled the horses.

Even with several days' rest he'd still reach Cavalon in time to defend himself in a Royal Court. Wearing himself and his horses out before a trial by combat was the last thing he wanted to do. Normally he would have joined the tourney, but he couldn't risk injuring himself with the accusation of treason hanging over him. The knight who'd falsely accused him would soon regret his words. Forcing the anger away, he settled in under the tree.

# *Chapter Two: Beatrice*

Beatrice stepped around a corner and nearly ran into two squires. She nodded in acceptance of their apologies before hurrying away. The castle and town had been overcrowded ever since her sister had told Meliance he needed to prove his love for her. Her father had called all their kith and kin to fight against Meliance and now they waited for the tourney to go ahead. She hoped it would be soon. Both her father and sister were annoyed with the council.

While looking for somewhere quiet, she had overheard servants saying Garin was on his way to visit her father to talk about the tourney. She wanted to hear what he had to say, but people kept getting in her way and slowing her down. Everyone listened to Garin and put great store in his words. If he said the tourney would go ahead, then it would. That'd please her sister and father who'd both been in a bad mood since the council had said no.

Avoiding a group of ladies standing around chatting. Beatrice tried to keep a pleasant smile on her face. When she was old enough for a suitor she wouldn't string him along like her sister was doing. If Claudine wasn't careful, she might lose Meliance to another lady. One who was more appreciative of him. She arrived in time to hear her father speak, annoyed to find she'd missed part of the conversation.

"Are you certain?"

Garin nodded. "Yes. I've been assured two Knights of the Round Table travel towards our town. We should go ahead with the tourney in the hope of winning riches from them. How can we not win with the amount of brave men willing to fight for us?"

Thiebault turned to his squire. "Inform the council that Garin advises we go ahead with the tourney."

With a nod, the lad scurried off.

Beatrice stepped out of the way, having paused in the doorway. Maybe the castle would soon return to normal and all those who'd arrived to fight in the tourney would go home. And hopefully her sister would finally accept Meliance and the poor knight could stop having to try so hard to please her. She could have told him that very little pleased her sister. It was a wonder he hadn't realised after being raised with them for so many years. She'd heard servants whisper love was blind and nod knowingly when they spoke of Claudine and Meliance. They were careful not to say it where Claudine might overhear. Not that she blamed them. Her sister could be cruel. Meliance was only the latest example.

A cluster of ladies walked towards the doorway, talking about finding a good viewing place to watch the tourney. Beatrice trailed behind them. They headed for the tower and when they reached the top, Beatrice nearly groaned to find her sister already there. She tried to stay out of sight and remain behind the group of ladies she'd followed. It didn't help.

Claudine smiled at Beatrice, one closer to a smirk. "If it isn't the maid with the narrow sleeves."

Beatrice didn't reply. It never helped, only had her sister teasing her further. She also refrained from running her hands along the old fashioned sleeves she preferred to wear, having had too many mishaps with the flowing sleeves that were currently in fashion. She hoped the fashions changed soon.

"Have you seen the knight resting under the oak tree, Claudine? I wonder who he is," one of the ladies said.

Claudine looked in the direction the lady pointed. "There are two shields and two horses, where is his companion?"

Relieved her sister's attention was no longer on her, Beatrice looked towards the knight the lady had pointed out. She saw the two shields hanging in the tree and his horses grazing nearby. Now that was what a knight should look like. Even sitting on the grass, leaning against the trunk of an oak tree, he looked ready for battle.

"I see no one else," said another lady.

"What would a knight want with two shields?" a third lady asked.

"Oh look, the tourney has begun. Isn't that your Meliance?" the first lady asked.

Beatrice's gaze remained on the unknown knight. Why did he remain there? Did he plan to join the tourney later? Was he waiting for someone? Her imagination was caught as she came up with all sorts of scenarios about the solitary knight.

Claudine gestured in the direction of Meliance. "Is there any fairer knight? Only look at him, ladies. Look how he carries himself." She sent a sideways glance towards Beatrice. "Far better than the knight that seems to have caught my sister's attention."

The other ladies tittered and Beatrice pressed her lips together in an effort to remain silent.

Claudine looked directly at Beatrice. "Not even so lowly a knight would be interested in you with your narrow sleeves."

Anger and humiliation rushed in on Beatrice. "He's a fairer knight than Meliance." If Claudine hadn't been so focused on making herself appear more important because of everything Meliance was doing for her, she would have been admiring the knight under the oak tree too.

Claudine went to strike her sister.

Beatrice scurried back, nearly tripping over the hem of her dress, afraid her sister would attack her.

Several of the ladies held Claudine, one saying, "Never mind her. What would she know? Only look at her sleeves."

She watched Claudine warily, wondering if she should back away further. She knew she shouldn't have said anything. It always made it worse. But the words stung. They always did.

Claudine's eyes narrowed and she pulled away from the ladies who held her. "You're right of course. She knows absolutely nothing. Forget her, we're missing the tourney."

Beatrice stared at her sister's back, forcing herself to ignore the hurtful words. She hoped Meliance lost. By doing so, he'd win an escape from Claudine. When her sister remained engrossed in the tourney, she crept forward, staying well away from Claudine so she could watch the tourney.

As it progressed lances were shivered, shields pierced and knights unhorsed. Meliance beat all who came at him. Those he didn't unseat with his lance, or if his lance broke, he attacked with his sword. None could stand against him.

Beatrice's attention was regularly drawn to the knight resting under the oak tree. Who was he? Why hadn't he joined the tourney? She'd thought he'd have joined in by now. He looked like he'd faced many a battle and his horses were in good shape. She couldn't understand why he wasn't participating. Was he hurt? Her gaze roved over his body, but she could see no sign of injury. He'd also appeared to move quite easily when he'd risen before to take food from his saddlebags. So why wasn't he joining the tourney? Her sister's voice interrupted her thoughts.

"Ladies, isn't he wonderful? Meliance is the best bachelor knight in all the lands and the minstrels will sing songs about this day and the effort he went to so he could win my hand. Isn't he the fairest and bravest of all those in the tourney?"

Fed up with listening to her sister's bragging and still hurting from the earlier words, Beatrice spoke before she could stop herself. "I see a handsomer knight. I like him far better than Meliance. He wouldn't last against the knight under the oak tree." That knight was far superior to her sister's suitor.

"How dare you be such a disrespectful child? I won't allow you to make such comments about Meliance. Show some respect to your elders." Claudine slapped her sister hard. "That'll teach you to behave better." She went to strike her again, but the ladies drew her away.

Beatrice glared at her sister. She hadn't expected her to move so fast. Feeling the heat of her cheek she was certain it showed the imprint of her sister's hand. Her sister wasn't that much older than her that she should discipline her or expect her to respect her as her elder. Before she could argue against Claudine's treatment of her, one of the ladies spoke.

"Why doesn't the knight beneath the oak tree take up arms?"

A second lady said, "Maybe he's sworn to keep the peace."

A third said, "He's a merchant bringing horses to market. He plans to sell that armour to the knights."

"You lie," Beatrice said. "He's a knight. Look at his clothes. Look at the way he holds himself. Do you think a merchant would carry lances like that? He looks like a knight, not a merchant."

One of the ladies laughed. "Oh you poor, sweet child, Beatrice. Just because he looks like a knight doesn't mean he is one. He's probably dressed as a knight to avoid the tariff. Instead he'll be found out and hung for a cheat."

I don't believe a word you've said. Anyone can see for themselves that he's a knight." She tried to ignore the laughter her words brought, her sister's laugh the loudest. No matter what she said or did, Claudine always found fault with it. If she'd agreed with her sister, then she would have been teased for having no idea what she spoke about, only parroting those around her. It wasn't fair how Claudine treated her.

# Chapter Three: Gawain

Gawain heard everything the ladies said in the tower, their words drifting down to him. It angered and shamed him that he couldn't prove them wrong. He also wished he could defend the young maiden who'd stood up for him and been struck for her efforts. If the accusation against him wasn't so terrible he would have taken part in the tourney. But he couldn't risk leaving his name forever smeared by the charge of treason should anything happen to him by joining in.

He remained under the oak tree, giving his horses the rest they deserved. The words the ladies spoke continued to drift down to him. One of them spoke constantly of Meliance and how great a knight he was. He suspected it was Claudine, the lady who'd caused the tourney. The one who'd defended him didn't speak again and he wondered if she'd left. He wouldn't blame her after all that had been said and done. The poor child. He wondered how old she was. She hadn't sounded overly young. She was probably on the verge of becoming a young lady herself.

Gawain sighed as he heard one of the ladies call out to a squire that was close to the tower. Had those ladies nothing better to do than cause trouble? Why would they ask the squire if he'd seen the knight under the oak tree? It was obvious they hadn't realised that with the wind travelling in his direction he could hear everything they said.

The squire looked in his direction. "I've seen him."

"He looks a great knight, but we've noticed he hasn't once stirred. Not even to defend himself," one lady said.

A second lady said, "He wouldn't stir if one plucked a hair from his beard. You could take his armour and treasure and none would stop you."

The squire looked towards him again.

Gawain hoped the squire would show some sense and walk away without listening to the troublesome ladies. After a few minutes, it was clear the squire had no sense.

The lad strode towards him and struck out at one of the horses. The horse trotted out of reach. "Are you sick that you've lain here all day long and done nothing?"

Gawain rose to his feet, glancing towards his horse before he focused his attention on the squire. "What is it to you why I tarry? Go about your business and stop meddling in mine."

The squire looked towards the tower where the ladies were and then eyed Gawain again. Gawain hoped the lad was bright enough to realise that following the suggestion of the ladies wouldn't be a good idea. Once more the squire glanced towards the ladies, who were currently silent, before he eyed Gawain up and down then ambled off. Gawain watched him go, waiting until he was out of sight before he made himself comfortable on the grass under the tree. He pitied poor young Meliance should he win the hand of Claudine. If someone caused him to lose they'd be doing him a favour. He doubted the shallow Claudine would be interested in Meliance should he fail to live up to her expectations.

Gawain remained under the tree until the tourney ended for the day, noticing how many horses were captured and the amount of knights that were killed. As much as it pained him to remain a spectator, he couldn't risk death or injury until he'd defended himself at the Royal Court. His family didn't deserve such a smear left on their good name should something happen to him on his journey to Cavalon.

After the combatants decided to meet again on the next day to continue the tourney, and wandered away, Gawain gathered up his gear and horses and headed for the small gate that had been locked earlier. He found it unlocked and made his way inside, having first stepped back to let an elderly nobleman through.

"Sir, let me offer you room in my home. You'll be lucky to find lodgings in the town with how many are here for the tourney."

Gawain thanked the nobleman and walked beside him through the streets, grateful for the offer of hospitality. He didn't doubt the town would be full and lodgings hard to come by with how many he'd seen at the tourney during the day.

The man introduced himself as Garin and talked of the events of the day, finally asking Gawain why he hadn't borne arms.

He guessed the man deserved an answer after offering him room for the night. "I'm honour bound to defend myself in a Royal Court against an accusation of treason. I can't risk myself in a tourney until I've freed myself from the allegations cast against me. It would dishonour not only myself, but also my friends and family if I didn't arrive in time."

Garin nodded. "You did the right thing. It'd be dishonourable to do anything else." They reached Garin's home and he called servants forward to see to the horses before turning to Gawain. "Come in and meet my family. I have two lovely daughters and a son, Herman. Join us for a meal. Afterwards though, I must leave for awhile to visit my lord, Thiebault."

"Thank you. I appreciate your offer of hospitality." Gawain followed him inside.

"Think nothing of it. I'm honoured to offer it to a worthy knight such as yourself. There'd be many who'd be caught up in the glory of the moment instead of remaining steadfast to their principles. You have my admiration."

Gawain nodded, not bothering to tell him how hard it had been. Particularly while he'd listened to the ladies mock Beatrice when she'd stood up for him. He owed that young maiden a favour and hoped one day he'd be able to repay her kind words. He'd travel back through here once he'd finished in Cavalon and see how she fared.

## *Chapter Four: Beatrice*

The meal was ended and Beatrice was about to leave, wanting to escape both her father's complaints about all he'd lost due to the tourney and her sister's bragging. She remained at the table when she heard her sister speak to their father.

"Sir, you haven't suffered a loss if only you'd take the goods a merchant brought to sell, disguising himself as a knight so he can avoid customs."

Beatrice stared at Claudine. Surely she didn't mean the knight who'd been under the oak tree. She couldn't help thinking about some of the accusations the ladies with her sister had made about him.

"What is this about?" Thiebault asked.

"There was a man resting under an oak tree near the tower all day. We thought him a knight with his palfreys, lances, armour and shields. I've since learned we were wrong. He's a merchant, disguised as a knight so he can avoid paying the tariff. It's all so he can sell his wares freely to those in the tourney tomorrow and it won't cost him a single extra coin," Claudine said.

Beatrice was horrified by her sister's words. She hadn't believed she'd take her spitefulness this far. "Father–"

Thiebault brushed her words aside

with a wave of his hand. "Hush, child. Your sister is speaking. Go on, Claudine."

"He deserves to be punished and have his wares confiscated for trying to cheat customs. You could take them for the good of the town, Father."

Beatrice shook her head. "But Father–"

Thiebault glared at her and she shrank back in her chair. "Quiet. How many times must I ask you to be silent?"

Beatrice dropped her gaze to her hands that rested on her lap, but not before she saw the sly smile her sister gave her.

"I saw him pass me by in the streets earlier, walking with Garin. That noble gentleman offered him a room for the night. He's tricked one of our most honourable townspeople. Who knows what else such a dishonourable man plans to do."

Thiebault rose to his feet. "I'll ride over there directly and see to the matter. Thank you for bringing this to my attention, Claudine." He strode from the room.

Beatrice stared after her father, trying to figure out what to do.

Claudine walked past her, pausing long enough to jeer, "We'll see how fair a knight he is after he's been thrown into prison."

She remained frozen in her seat as her sister stepped through the doorway. She had to warn him. Jumping to her feet, she raced from the room. It was difficult to slip quietly from the castle with the amount of people currently residing there. She eventually managed to leave by a back gate and raced down the hill to Garin's home. His two daughters greeted her and she struggled to hide her impatience.

"Our father's barely left to visit yours. We begged to go with him so we could visit with you," the oldest girl said.

"And here you are." The younger one giggled. "To think we might have missed you if we'd gone with him."

"My father is on the way here to visit yours." Beatrice looked in the direction her father would come from. She'd half expected him to be here already. "He's coming to see the knight you have staying with you."

"Oh, he's splendid." The oldest girl sighed dramatically.

"He told us about some of the most

marvellous adventures he's had," the younger one said.

Beatrice wanted to demand they take her to him, but knew that would shock them. They'd be full of questions she couldn't answer. Not without shaming her family. If only they hadn't spotted her when she'd arrived. Then she could have snuck in and warned the knight.

"Oh, here they come now." The oldest girl pointed behind Beatrice.

She turned to see her father riding towards them with Garin and Herman. It was too late. "I must go." She slipped off into the shadows, not wanting to risk her father finding her there. Before she'd gone far, their words brought her to a stop.

"I have no idea who told you my guest is a merchant, but you'll soon see he's a fair and noble knight,"

Garin said. "Even to speak so against my guest dishonours my house and my family name."

"I have no wish to bring dishonour to you or yours, but I must make sure your guest is who he claims to be. That he's not a merchant planning to sell horses and avoid the tariff as has been suggested," Thiebault said.

The relief Beatrice felt at hearing Garin's words was short lived. Knowing Claudine, she wouldn't let the matter go until she felt the knight had been sufficiently punished for having appeared to be a better knight than her own suitor. There had to be a way to bring an end to her spitefulness. Without the knight paying the price. She wished now she'd held her tongue and not said anything. Although she doubted that would have made a difference. Maybe if her sister hadn't seen her looking at him admiringly that might have helped.

Her gaze was drawn to the narrow sleeves of her dress, barely visible in the shadows where she hid. She was so tired of her sister's taunting and the way the ladies followed her lead. Somehow she needed to undo the trouble she'd accidentally caused the knight by both noticing and defending him. She should have known better than to say anything to her sister, but sometimes she couldn't help it. Her sister made her so angry and her words stung so badly they nearly brought her to tears.

# Chapter Five: Gawain

Gawain was seated by the fire, considering retiring for the night, when his host returned with another guest. He rose to his feet. "Welcome."

Once greetings were over, they all seated themselves by the fire and Garin asked Gawain to tell Thiebault all he'd told him earlier. Gawain nodded, unable to refuse not only his host, but the lord of the country.

Once the tale was told, Thiebault said, "That is more than sufficient an excuse, but tell me, where is the battle to be held?"

"Sir, before the King of Cavalon. It's where I travel to now."

"I'll guide you and provide you with food and pack animals to carry it since you must travel through a poor country," Garin said.

"Thank you for your kind offer, Sir," Gawain said. "It's extremely generous, but one that's unnecessary. I've travelled this way before and I'll have food and lodgings if it can be bought."

They talked a little longer until Thiebault said he must return home and Gawain and Garin walked outside with him to where his horse waited for him.

A young girl dashed out of the shadows. "Sir, I beseech you to help me. I've come to complain of my sister who struck me, not for the first time, and seek justice."

Gawain recognised the voice, but he had no idea why she should come to him looking for justice. Before he had a chance to say anything, Thiebault stepped forward, taking his daughter by the arm.

"Who bid you to come and complain to this knight? What is this nonsense about your sister? Go home, child."

Gawain saw the tears form in the girl's eyes as she tried to pull away from Thiebault. "Is this your daughter, Sir?"

"Yes, to my shame it is."

"Let her speak. I would hear what she has to say." He owed her that much at least for her kind words and defence of him that afternoon.

"If you wish, but don't pay too much mind to the silly girl."

With a nod for Thiebault, Gawain turned his attention to Beatrice. There was a shimmer of tears in her eyes, but they didn't diminish the look of determination that was also there. "Speak, child. I'll hear what you have to say."

"I wish to complain about my sister. After today, I don't love her anymore and I fear she's never thought kindly of me. Several times she struck out at me and once she hit me hard enough to leave behind the imprint of her hand. She's done me a great shame for your sake."

Wanting to know all the details, particularly to find out if there was something that had occurred after the tourney had ended for the day, Gawain asked, "What have I to do with what your sister has done against you and how can I offer you justice for it?"

"Pay no attention to the foolish child. It will only be some sisterly quarrel," Thiebault said.

"How could I continue to call myself a knight if I ignored a maiden in distress? It would be churlish of me." Particularly if he was to ignore a maiden he was indebted to, but he didn't want to mention that and shame her even further by letting her know he'd heard all that had happened in the tower. "What is it you wish me to do?"

"If it pleases you Sir, I'd have you bear arms for me in the tourney."

"Have you ever made this petition of any knight before?" Gawain asked.

"No, Sir." Beatrice shook her head.

"Pay no attention to the foolish

child," Thiebault said. "You have more important things to do than settle the quarrel of my daughters."

He stared at Beatrice, seeing not only hurt and determination in her expression, but also fear. He turned to Thiebault. "I will not refuse your daughter." Gawain's gaze shifted from Thiebault to Beatrice. "If you wish it, I'll be your knight in the tourney tomorrow and gain you the justice you seek." He'd repay the favour he owed her for coming to his defence. It looked like she was sorely in need of someone to defend her. And with the cruelty of her sister it was no wonder.

"I do wish it, Sir."

After more words, they parted and Gawain watched as Thiebault rode away, his daughter on his Palfrey in front of him.

"It seems an insignificant matter to risk yourself and your reputation for," Garin said.

Gawain turned to the man standing beside him. "As a knight I should be willing to risk myself not only for great glory, but also for the things that I know are right no matter how small or insignificant they seem. How could I turn down the first plea for justice a young lady has made?" He continued to keep to himself her defence of him, not wanting to shame her further by talking about the way her sister and the ladies had mocked her. The lass deserved better treatment than that. As too did Meliance of Lis.

# Chapter Six: Beatrice

Beatrice leaned back against her father as his horse walked up the hill towards the castle. She could barely believe the knight had agreed to fight for her honour in the tourney. But she shouldn't have been surprised. She'd known at once that he was a great knight. Far greater than Meliance.

"What brought you out into the night to bother Garin's guest?"

She turned so she could see her father. Was he finally going to listen to what she had to say instead of telling her to be quiet? "Earlier today I was annoyed with Claudine who wouldn't believe there was any knight better than Meliance. When I defended the knight resting underneath the oak tree not far from our tower, she struck out at me. Her and her ladies made up all sorts of false accusations about him and when I continued to say he was a better knight than Meliance she hit me hard enough to leave a mark."

"Was the knight close enough to have heard all of this?"

Beatrice shook her head. "I don't believe so." She paused a moment. "I hope he shows Claudine tomorrow how wrong she is in saying there's no greater knight than Meliance of Lis."

"I dare say you're correct, but we'll find out for certain tomorrow. Why didn't you come to me with your grievance instead of bothering the knight?"

"I tried. You told me to be silent."

Thiebault remained quiet for a moment. "You should send him a token he can take in the tourney tomorrow. A sleeve or a wimple."

Beatrice looked at her narrow sleeves and felt ashamed at her inability to wear more fashionable ones. "I'd like to send him a token, but I can't think he'd like a sleeve as small and narrow as mine."

"I'll think on it and find something more suitable for you to send him."

"Thank you." She sat contentedly before her father, wondering what he'd think of for her to send as a token.

When they arrived at the castle, Claudine strode over to them.

"Where did you find my sister? What tricks has she been up to now?"

"What is it to you?" When Claudine tried to answer him, Thiebault interrupted her. "Hush. It grieves me to hear how you behaved today. You were discourteous and rude to your sister. I'm sorely disappointed. To make matters worse, you made false accusations against an honourable man."

Claudine opened her mouth several times to protest during her father's words, but in the end she fled without speaking.

Beatrice stared after her sister, while her father turned his attention to one of his people. Never before had she seen Claudine speechless. Her sister always had something to say and usually something nasty. Drawing her gaze from the doorway her sister had disappeared through, she noticed her father had set some of his people to working on a piece of red samite.

She moved closer so she could see more clearly what they were doing with the heavy silk fabric that was woven with threads of gold. They were stitching together a long, wide sleeve they'd cut from the fabric.

Thiebault came to stand beside her. "Rise early tomorrow morning. Take this token to your knight so he can wear it in the tourney and all will see he battles on your behalf."

She couldn't take her gaze from the luxurious fabric. Any knight would be proud to carry such a magnificent token. "Thank you. I'll take it to him the moment the sun rises."

Even though she asked everyone to wake her with the dawn, Beatrice struggled to fall asleep, worried she'd sleep in. She was the first one to rise the next morning and, gathering the sleeve, headed through the back gate and down the hill to Garin's house.

She arrived to find all the knights of the household had risen earlier than her and had gone to the monastery to hear the mass sung. She waited for them to return. The moment she saw Gawain, she ran to greet him, holding out the sleeve. "I'd be honoured if you carried this token with you on the field today."

"I'd be pleased to wear your token so all know I battle for justice on your behalf." Gawain took the sleeve she held out to him.

With a deep curtsy, and more thanks, Beatrice hurried away, sending several glances over her shoulder at the knight who watched her leave. Returning to the tower she'd watched the tourney from yesterday, she found it crowded with her sister and the ladies who'd also been there. They chatted amongst themselves as they pointed out various knights on the field.

"There's Meliance, the most chivalrous knight of them all," Claudine said.

Beatrice wasn't about to let her say one more nasty comment about her knight. Especially not since he rode forth in her name. "No, the knight about to face Meliance is the most chivalrous one."

Claudine raised her hand. "How dare you."

Beatrice took a step away. "We'll soon see who has the right of the matter. The knight who fights your Meliance is the one who fights for me. Don't you see the red samite sleeve I gave him as a token?"

Claudine laughed. "All can see that isn't one of your sleeves. It's too long and flowing."

"Father had it made for me to give specially to him."

"Look, they ride towards each other," one of the ladies exclaimed.

Beatrice stared at her knight, her hands clasped together in front of her as she held her breath. The two knights galloped towards each other, lances aimed at shields.

"What did I tell you?" Claudine demanded. "Is there anyone braver than Meliance? He isn't trying to avoid that lance."

The knight's lance shivered against Meliance's shield from the force of the blow, launching Meliance from his saddle. Meliance lay unmoving on the field. Claudine shrieked as the knight took the reins of Meliance's charger and gave them to a varlet.

Beatrice couldn't hear what the knight said to the serving boy, but the lad nodded his head and led the charger towards the tower. She turned to her sister. "There lies Meliance, who you praised so highly." She gestured towards Meliance who was now being helped from the field by his squire. "You see, I was right when I said yesterday that I saw a better knight."

"Hold your tongue or I'll slap you," Claudine snarled.

"You'd strike me for telling the truth, as you did yesterday?"

"You deserved it." Claudine tried to strike her sister, but the ladies held her back.

"I asked the knight to fight against

Meliance for me. To seek justice for the way you treated me yesterday. It's clear by how easily he won that you were in the wrong," Beatrice said.

"You lie." Again Claudine tried to attack Beatrice and once more the ladies stopped her. "No one would fight for you with your narrow sleeves and constant lies."

The varlet called up to them. "The knight sends Meliance's charger to the young lady, Beatrice, being the first of the spoils gained in the tourney he fights on her behalf."

Silence fell around Beatrice and she smiled down at the boy. "Thank you. Could you see that the horse is taken care of and stabled for me?" When the boy nodded and led the charger away, she turned to her sister. "Who is the one who lies?"

With a shriek, Claudine pulled

away from the ladies that held her and stormed from the tower. A momentary silence was left in her wake.

One of the ladies turned to Beatrice. "That was a fine charger your knight presented you with." Several of them murmured in agreement.

Beatrice inclined her head, turning to watch the tourney in time to see the knight give the reins of another horse to a varlet. The servant led the animal from the field. She smiled as she heard the conversations around her. They were far different from those of yesterday. Today it was her knight they were praising, not Claudine's.

# Chapter Seven: Gawain

Gawain rode into the town, the tourney over. He'd won four horses. The first one he'd given to Beatrice, the second to Garin's wife for her hospitality and the other two he'd kept for his own family. Around him people congratulated him on his feats and some called out asking who he was. Remaining silent, only giving the occasional nod in thanks, he continued to ride to Garin's home. He planned to gather his gear and continue his journey. There was enough light left in the day that he should reach an abbey he knew of before dark.

When he arrived at the gates of Garin's home, he saw Beatrice waited for him. He dismounted to stand before her.

Beatrice dropped into a low curtsy. "I want to thank you for fighting in the tourney for me."

"If I can ever be of service to you again, only send me a message." He bowed to her, thinking of the young knight he'd unhorsed. He doubted Meliance would thank him if it cost him the lady he loved, but from all he'd heard, the young man would be far better off without her.

Thiebault joined them. "Let me add my thanks to those of my daughter's. To whom should I offer these thanks? You never did tell me your name."

"Sir, it was never my intention to conceal my name. You never once asked it before this moment. I'm Sir Gawain, one of King Arthur's knights." He heard the cries of surprise and exclamations that ran through the crowd and watched as Thiebault's expression changed. This was why he didn't offer his name unless asked.

"Sir Gawain, let me offer you lodgings this evening. Allow me to show you proper honour for all you've done for Beatrice."

"Thank you, but I plan to ride on since there's still quite a few hours of daylight left." When Thiebault continued to urge him to stay, Gawain remained firm in his plans. The crowd started to thin as people called out their congratulations and bid him farewell. Soon it was only Garin, Thiebault and Beatrice left. Gawain mounted his horse. "I had best take my leave if I wish to travel any great distance before sunset."

Beatrice came forward and curtsied low again, this time dropping a kiss on his foot.

"What made you do that?" He stared down at the maiden, with her arms encased in their old fashioned sleeves.

"So that no matter where you travel, you'll never forget me." She smiled up at him.

Gawain returned her smile. "I could never forget you, my friend. I never forget those who come to my defence." He watched as her smile wavered, to be replaced by surprise, then returned even brighter than before. "Take care my friend, and remember to send a message if you should have need of me."

"I will." Beatrice took a step back from him, continuing to smile.

He rode his horse towards Garin's house, looking over his shoulder after a moment. This time it was only Beatrice there, her father and Garin having left. She raised her hand and waved, still smiling at him.

He lifted his hand in farewell before he faced forward again, glad he'd fought in the tourney. Not for glory, but for honour and justice.

# Princess Ilse, The Giant's Daughter

Ilse's father is willing to do anything to keep her from the man she loves. She doesn't care he's a mortal. She's willing to do anything to prevent her father from keeping them apart. Although things aren't going exactly the way she'd hoped.

*

People have been telling stories since the beginning of time. Fairytales, folklore, myths and legends are among some of the stories that have been told over and over through the centuries. The basic story remains the same, but each storyteller adds their own style, sometimes adding something unique to the tale.

*

This story was written by an Australian author using Australian spelling.

# Princess Ilse, The Giant's Daughter

Princess Ilse slipped out of her father's Castle, glancing numerous times over her shoulder. If she had to listen to one more word from the boring knights her father preferred, she was likely to push one of them down the mountain. Why couldn't he understand she was only interested in Ralf, the Lord of Westerberg? What did it matter that she was a giant and he a mortal?

She sighed heavily before once

again glancing over her shoulder. It seemed that no one had noticed she'd left. It was getting harder and harder to come up with original excuses as to what she was doing and where she was going. The knights were easily fooled. Her father wasn't. If only he wasn't so stubborn, then she wouldn't have to sneak off all the time. She wondered how long it would take him to realise she'd left. Telling the knight she'd been talking to, 'excuse me a moment' wasn't going to buy her much time. He'd probably look for her soon. But she was sick of making up excuses and had drawn a blank when she'd tried to think of one to use. It didn't matter. She didn't need a lot of time to cover enough ground to be well out of sight before they started looking for her.

She continued to stride across the

land, giving up checking over her shoulder every few seconds once she was far enough away. Glancing at the position of the sun she saw it was well past the middle of the day and hoped Ralf still waited for her. It was a wonder he continued to try and meet her with how often she'd been unable to see him at agreed upon times.

When she reached the glade where they were to meet, she was relieved to find Ralf waiting for her. He rose to his feet when he saw her, smiling. She hurried forward. "I'm sorry it took me so long to get here."

"I feared you wouldn't be able to come today. And when the time we'd agreed upon passed I couldn't bring myself to leave, hoping I'd still see you."

She sat down so she wouldn't

tower over him, even though he'd told her many times her height didn't bother him. "My father grows more difficult. If we ran away we wouldn't have this problem. We could find somewhere far from here to live. Where no one knows us and my father wouldn't be able to keep us apart. Where we could see each other for more than a few stolen moments every few days."

"You can't imagine how many times I've thought the same. Yet I couldn't desert the people of Westerberg. As deeply as I care for you, I couldn't be so selfish. They depend on me."

She sighed heavily, reminding herself it was one of the things she loved about him. His care for his people. "Of course you're right." She only wished he wasn't. Wished the two of them were unimportant and could follow their hearts.

"Put it from your mind. We're together for now. I don't want to waste a moment of our time on things that can't be." He placed his hand over hers where it rested on the ground. "I for one am grateful to see you today when I feared I wouldn't."

She smiled. No wonder every knight her father presented to her, in the hope she'd find one interesting, left her wondering how soon she could escape his attention. None of them could compare to Ralf. "You're right. Again."

Ralf chuckled. "If only my advisors felt the same way."

"What are they arguing about this time?"

They spent the next few hours talking together and as the sun dropped closer to the mountain, Ilse couldn't stop looking towards it, willing it to slow its descent. The time she spent with Ralf always raced by, never seeming long enough. Eventually she had to bid him farewell and after making another time to meet, she trudged home.

Her father met her at the door of the castle, towering over her. "Where have you been?" His booming voice echoed around the courtyard.

He'd never once believed any of the excuses she'd used so she'd stopped trying to think of new ones. "I grew bored with the knights you invited."

"You were visiting with that mortal again, weren't you?"

Ilse glared at her father. She had no idea how he'd learned about Ralf, but he'd known from the first. "What if I was? You can't force me to love one of those knights you invited here today." There was no way she could push past him to get into the castle. As large as she was, her father was even larger. He was probably the largest giant living.

"Then I'll invite others. Poems have been written about your beauty. Songs have been sung. How can you think of wasting yourself on a mere mortal? I won't allow it. He is beneath you. Unworthy of your attention."

She wanted to argue against his words, but there was no point. She would be wasting her breath. He hadn't listened to a single word she'd spoken in Ralf's defence. "Are you going to let me inside or stand there all night barring the entrance?"

"Did you hear me?"

"The entire valley probably heard you."

"You will not see him again. Understand?" He jabbed a finger in her direction.

"I'm not simple. I understand you perfectly." Just because she understood him, didn't mean she was going to follow his orders. The thought of never seeing Ralf again caused an ache in her chest.

"I'll invite other knights. Ones worthy of your beauty and position. You'll find an appropriate suitor and forget the mortal you pine after. You'll soon see he is nothing compared to the knights I'll show you. And you will never see him again." Jabbing his finger in her direction one last time, he turned and strode into the castle.

Ilse stared after him. He could

invite whoever he pleased, but that didn't mean she'd find them any more interesting than the previous guests. There was no way she'd let him stop her from seeing Ralf. If only her father could understand how deeply she cared for him. She couldn't imagine her life without Ralf and she was certain he felt the same way. Her father might as well rip her heart from her body than to keep her from Ralf. It would feel the same.

Entering the castle, she thought back over her afternoon. Her lips slowly curved into a smile and her steps slowed. She couldn't wait to see him again. They were to meet in the glade at midday tomorrow. After he'd taken care of the running of his lands and dealt with all the problems his advisors were always finding for him. She'd be counting the hours until she saw him. And no one, not her father or any of the knights he kept introducing her to, were going to keep her from seeing Ralf.

The hours passed slowly the next day and once again Ilse was forced to endure the company of the knights her father had invited. Not a single one of them caught her attention. She doubted they were any more interested in her than she was in them. They only wanted to marry the daughter of the most powerful giant. She could have been ugly and they would have praised her as a great beauty. As it grew close to midday, she excused herself from the knight she spoke to and snuck out of the castle to spend the rest of the day with Ralf. This time she wasn't late.

Day after day, she continued to meet up with Ralf, spending as much time as possible with him. Each afternoon when she returned home, her father would demand that she stop seeing him. Yelling at her so his voice thundered around the valley. She didn't bother arguing with him and stood there listening to his demands and lectures, all the time glaring at him and wishing he'd leave her alone. She dreamt about escaping her father's house, knowing that until he gave up trying to find her a different suitor there would be no escape for her. As long as she stayed in the area, he'd hunt her down and drag her home. If only Ralf didn't have his people to take care of.

One morning she woke and, after readying herself for the day, she went looking for the knights her father had invited. There were none and she couldn't find her father. For a moment she stood there, stunned. Why were there no knights? Had he given up? Excitement raced through her. Surely he hadn't given up this quickly. She'd expected it to take a year at least. Another search of the castle showed that only the servants were about and none of them had any idea where her father was.

Grinning, she strode from the castle, planning to reach the glade before Ralf. She couldn't wait to tell him about this new development. She hadn't gone far when she saw her father. The excitement she'd felt disappeared, replaced by horror. She ran towards him. He was tearing into the land.

"Stop. What are you doing?" She grabbed hold of one of his arms and tried to prevent him from gouging out more of the land.

He shook her from him. "You wouldn't listen. I told you again and again the mortal wasn't for you. You deserve far better than that insignificant creature. You rejected all the knights I introduced you to. Shortly you'll have no choice. Once I finish, there'll be no way for you to reach the mortal. Then you will take proper notice of the next lot of knights I invite."

"No. Please, don't do this to us." She felt tears form and tried to hold them back. It was impossible. "I can't live without him." Her chest ached like someone had gouged great chunks from it. "Please, Father."

"You will forget him in time." He turned away from her and started tearing at the land again with his large hands.

She tried to stop him, but it was

impossible. He ripped up the land, creating a great gap between their mountain and the lands below. Every time she grabbed at his arms or tried to push boulders back into place, he set her aside or shook her from him. Tears ran down her cheeks and her pleading was ignored. Nothing she did or said stopped the gap from increasing.

When he was finished, he stood on the edge of the land and surveyed his work. Water raged through the great gap he'd created. Dusting off his hands, he faced Ilse. "You wouldn't listen. What else could I do?"

She stared after her father as he strode towards the castle. The tears dried, replaced by anger, the ache in her chest remaining. She wasn't about to let this stop her. Standing on the edge, she stared at the raging waters below. There had to be a way across. She raised her gaze to the land on the other side of the chasm. Surely she could reach the other side. She wasn't going to let her father keep her from Ralf. She couldn't live with the ache that tore at her chest. Looking in the direction of the castle, she eyed the ground. Maybe if she took a running leap it would be enough force to carry her across the chasm. She looked back and forth between the ground she prepared to run across and the chasm she wanted to vault over.

Each time her gaze was drawn to the raging waters below. Jumping was the only way she could reach the other side. It would be impossible to climb down, swim across the swiftly flowing waters and climb back up the other side. She stared at the land she wanted to reach, determination filling her. No one was going to keep her from Ralf. She'd show her father that he was going to have to try harder than that if he wanted to separate them.

Maybe it was time to convince Ralf to leave his people. As much as she admired how he cared for them, it might be the only way they could be together. With one last look at the raging waters below, she turned and trudged up the hill towards the castle. She stopped well before she reached it and turned around. Taking a deep breath, she ran towards the chasm. The downward slope helped her pick up speed and her hair streamed out behind her as she reached the torn up land.

She flung herself through the air and saw the other side coming closer and closer. For a second she thought she'd made it before she plummeted into the churning water below. As the cold, raging water rushed up around her, she feared it was the end. Thoughts of Ralf filled her mind, her longing for him mingled with sorrow at deserting him. Instead of drowning, like she'd expected, she felt herself change. She shot to the surface and looked down at herself as she tread in the foaming water, able to hold her own against the current. Her skin had a green cast to it and between her fingers was now webbed, her body sleek and small.

She was no longer a giant, having become instead an undine. A soulless creature forced to live in rivers and lakes. "No!" The word rang out around her, the sound of her voice unrecognisable. Her rage had sounded lyrical, her own familiar tones lost. Several more times she called out, lyrical words echoing around her. Words that sounded like they belonged to someone else.

By the time her father came looking for her, the waters had slowed some. She swam up and down the river as her father paced back and forth, calling her name. Anger churned through her, like the water rushing through the rocks. He didn't deserve an answer. Not after what he'd done. She remained silent like she had so many times as he'd lectured her about seeing Ralf, demanding she never see him again. When her father peered over the edge of the cliff he'd created, she sank beneath the water and waited for him to leave. He stood there for long drawn out moments, eventually turning away.

Breaking the surface she stared up

at the darkening sky, alone again. She could hear her father heading off into the distance, calling for her as he returned to the castle. He may have prevented her from visiting Ralf, but he'd also given her the means to escape his rule. There would be no more parade of knights for her to choose a suitor from. Nor would she ever tell him where she was so he could find other ways to ruin her life.

She would wait. One day Ralf would come looking for her when she no longer met with him in the glade. His love for her would have him seeking her out. She dived under the water, swimming upstream a fair distance before she broke the surface again. Immortality had its benefits. She would have all the time she needed to wait and plenty to spare.

Opening her mouth to call for Ralf,

in case he had ventured nearby looking for her, the words came out as a song. An enticing song calling him to join her, longing filling each sound. Next time she saw him, she'd convince him to leave his people behind and join her. Reaching the end of the song, she dived beneath the water, bursting out of it further upstream. Again she sang the enticing song, calling to her love. She knew, without a doubt, that if he heard the song he wouldn't be able to resist joining her. No one would.

# Ion, Son Of Apollo

Ion was raised by the Delphic priestess after being abandoned on the temple steps. He grows up believing Apollo favours him, but when he learns Apollo wants him to leave behind the only life he's ever known, and the woman who has raised him, he wishes he could reject the path Apollo has chosen for him. But the gods can be both kind and cruel and he wouldn't be the only one who suffers if he refuses. Unknown to Ion, the path Apollo sets him on could uncover secrets from his past. Secrets that if they'd been discovered when he was born would have led to his death.

*

People have been telling stories since the beginning of time. Fairytales, folklore, myths and legends are among some of the stories that have been told over and over through the centuries. The basic story remains the same, but each storyteller adds their own style, sometimes adding something unique to the tale.

*

This story was written by an Australian author using Australian spelling.

# Name Pronunciation

Like many names there is more than one way to pronounce the following ones. These are the pronunciations used in this story.

Aeolas (ee-or-lus)

Creusa (cray-oh-sah)

Delphi (dell-fie)

Delphic (dell-fic)

Erechtheus (eh-reck-thee-as)

Euobeans (you-bee-ans)

Ion (eye-on)

Pythia (pith-ee-uh)

Xuthus (zoh-thus)

# *Chapter One: Creusa*

Creusa stared down at her newborn son where he lay in the wicker basket she'd placed him in. He smiled up at her, his hands waving energetically, his soft brown eyes staring trustingly up at her. She looked away, blinking back tears. If her father, King Erechtheus, should learn she'd given birth he probably wouldn't believe he was the sun god's child and kill both her and the infant.

She forced herself to look at the child again. He had her dark coloured hair, but it was too soon to tell if it would be straight like her own, or fall in curls like the golden locks of his father. The child gurgled and she forced herself to hang golden charms around his neck rather than pick him up and hold him close. It was the best she could do for him. Rising to her feet, she lifted the wicker basket and carried him into the nearby cave. She could only pray someone found him and raised him as their own.

Placing the basket in the cave, in a sheltered place out of the sun and wind, she once again found herself staring down at him. She hadn't even been able to bring herself to name the child. If she had, she knew she wouldn't have been able to part with him. "Keep him safe." Her words were a whisper. "Protect your son, Apollo, and see that he's raised by someone who'll love and care for him." There were more words she wanted to speak. Words to beg Apollo to find a way for her to keep the child, but she knew it was impossible. She clasped her hands together in an effort not to reach for him again. It took several minutes before she could drag her gaze from the child.

Turning away, she left the cave and walked back along the narrow track. Her head was bowed and tears silently fell. "Keep him safe." She was unable to resist saying the words again. When she returned home she'd go to Apollo's temple and beseech him to answer her prayers. She'd leave offerings for him and ask him to look after their child and let her know he was safe. Surely he'd protect his son.

# Chapter Two: Ion

"Ion!"

He turned to face the young boy who ran towards him, pausing in his task of sweeping the temple steps. "Is something wrong?"

The boy shook his head. "The Delphic priestess wishes to see you. Immediately."

"Do you know what she wants?"

The boy shrugged.

"No matter. I'll find out soon enough." With a smile of thanks for the boy, Ion handed him the laurel broom and went to find his foster mother.

When he found her, his foster mother smiled up at him and patted the space beside her on the seat. He joined her, wondering what had brought the sorrowful look to her face that even her smile hadn't completely banished. "What's wrong?"

"The gods can be both kind and cruel, but never turn away from them, mock them or forget their existence as they can be jealous and punish those they believe deserve it." She reached for his hand, holding it in one and patting it with the other.

Dread filled him as his gaze was drawn to their hands. How many times had he seen her do this when she had bad news to impart? He met her gaze. "Did something happen?"

Her smile remained tinged with sorrow as she shook her head. "Not yet. But it will. Apollo came to me in a dream and told me it was time to let you go. You have your own path to follow and today it will be shown to you."

"I've trained my entire life to serve here at the temple, with you. I've never wanted anything else." How could he repay her for all she'd done if Apollo sent him away?

"The morning I found you on the temple steps, in your little wicker basket, I couldn't resist taking you in and raising you as my own. Every day I've thanked Apollo for giving you to me. I'll grieve every day after you leave, but I wouldn't change the joys I've experienced raising you, to avoid the sorrows that are to come."

"Then I won't go. There's nothing

that can make me leave here if I choose not to."

She laughed softly. "So fierce. There must be great warriors amongst your ancestors."

"No one, not even the gods can make me leave."

She patted his hand again. "Don't reject Apollo. I, more than most, know how terribly that would end. Promise me you won't reject him. You might be willing to face his wrath, but I'm not. Do you think he would punish only you?"

His anger evaporated. He'd do anything she asked of him, no matter how little he wished to do it. Without her he would have perished as an infant. She'd been there for him when his own parents had discarded him. It took a moment before he could force himself to speak the words he knew he needed to say. "I'll do what you ask."

"I know you will. You have always been an obedient son." She chuckled. "Apart from a few mischievous adventures when you were younger."

He smiled like he knew she expected of him when all the time he wanted to beg her not to desert him too. "When do I need to leave?"

"I don't know, but I'm sure you'll recognise the path when Apollo shows it to you. Don't be angry with him. Apollo has protected you all your life. You must be special to him. Why else would you have been left on the steps of his temple for me to find?"

He'd heard his entire life how much Apollo must favour him. He didn't feel very favoured at the moment. Where would the unknown path take him? Why couldn't he stay at the temple? Surely he could serve Apollo just as well here as anywhere else.

"Go ready your things and pray before the statue of Apollo. Remember to leave him an offering in thanks for all he's done and all he plans to do for you."

He nodded, knowing that if he spoke he might beg her to let him stay. The temple had been his home nearly his entire life. Drawing away from his foster mother, he rose to his feet. He started to turn away, his jaw tightening on the words that wanted to escape.

"I know you're disappointed and probably angry as well as scared, but don't be. Apollo will watch over you as long as you remain true to him." She smiled, this one not as sad as the previous ones. "Maybe one day you'll return to Delphi to consult the oracle."

"I will." His words were fierce. He wouldn't desert the one person who'd never deserted him. He held her gaze a moment longer before going to do her bidding.

It didn't take him long to pack his handful of belongings. He left them in his room on his kline bed. Thanking Apollo took a lot longer. Once that was done, he decided to watch those who'd come to ask his foster mother their questions for Apollo.

The first time he'd seen her in the role of The Pythia he'd been terrified. Not at first. To start with she'd only been his mother. She'd burned laurel leaves and barley meal upon the altar before she'd sat on the tripod. Upon her head had been a crown of bay leaves and she'd held a sprig of bay. But for all the trappings of a priestess, she'd still been the one who'd rocked him to sleep when he was young, told him stories of the gods and goddesses and taught him right from wrong.

When she'd become Apollo's mouthpiece he'd barely recognised her. The change had terrified him and he'd feared he'd lost his mother. Afterwards she'd been drained and exhausted, but once she'd rested she'd brushed away his worries telling him not to fear the gods. They helped those they favoured and Apollo favoured him greatly.

He arrived in time to hear an older man say, "I am Xuthus, son of Aeolas, and this is my wife Creusa, daughter of Erechtheus, the king of Athens. We have been married for numerous years and are grieved by the fact our union has never been blessed by children. We would like to ask Apollo what we should do about this matter and have brought great offerings in the hope of receiving an answer."

Ion felt a chill as he heard his foster mother speak. She was no longer the soft spoken woman who'd raised him. Instead, she spoke with the authority of Apollo. Once he'd gotten past his initial fear, watching her become the Delphic Oracle had always awed him. Today was no different.

"You should regard the first person you meet upon leaving this sanctuary, your son."

The words hit him like a physical blow. Ion backed away. He had to run before they left or he'd be the first one to meet them when they left the sanctuary. Hurrying away he stumbled, tripping over his own feet and sprawling on the steps where he'd been left as a baby. Rising to his feet, he heard a noise behind him. He turned, freezing when his gaze fell on Xuthus and Creusa. He was too late. Running was out of the question.

"Are you hurt? What happened?" Xuthus asked.

Ion shrugged. "I'm fine. I have no idea what happened. I'm not usually so clumsy."

Xuthus grinned. "It is as the Oracle predicted. The gods have sent you to be a blessing and a comfort in my old age. I'll be honoured to call such a handsome youth, son."

"Sir–"

"No need to protest. The gods will it. What's your name?"

Ion looked from one to the other.

Both were smiling at him. He thought of his foster mother who'd made him promise to accept the path that would take him away from her. He had no choice. His shoulders slumped. "Ion."

"Gather your possessions, Ion. We leave immediately."

He wanted to protest that he couldn't leave until his foster mother had finished seeing all the people who'd come to ask questions of Apollo. He wanted to say goodbye to her. But he'd promised. With a heavy heart, he nodded and went to gather his possessions.

# Chapter Three: Creusa

Creusa was about to join her husband, who was talking to one of his friends, when she heard him mention Ion's name. She stepped back out of view and stopped to listen.

"It wouldn't surprise me if the boy was mine. Why else would the gods have directed me to him? The oracle did say I should regard the first person I met as my son."

"Who would his mother be?"

Xuthus shrugged. "Some serving girl I suppose."

"Well he does have your colouring."

Xuthus chuckled. "And the colouring of nearly everyone else here. Its common enough."

"No, it's a slightly richer, darker shade than the rest of us."

"It might have been once, before I started to go grey. But it's not that unique a colour. Even my wife has a similar shade. As do many members of my family. It doesn't matter who his parents were. The gods have given Ion to me. He's my son. I should have realised Creusa was the reason there's been no child born of our union."

She couldn't listen to another word and hurried to her chamber. Was Ion her husband's son to another woman?

And a base born one at that. Did he ever plan to tell her or did he expect her to remain in ignorance? He hadn't needed to go to all this trouble to find them a son. If he'd only asked, she would have accepted a child of his that had been born before they were married. She thought fleetingly of her own son she'd abandoned so many years ago. She pushed the thought firmly from her mind, refusing to give into the sorrow that swamped her every time she allowed herself to dwell on him. The tears came anyway, tainted by the bitterness she felt at the words she'd heard her husband speak.

"Mistress?"

Startled, she turned to see a servant, one who'd served her family faithfully since before she'd been born. She dashed the tears from her face. She'd been so caught up in her thoughts she hadn't noticed him tidying her chamber.

"Can I help you, mistress?"

She shook her head, wiping at the tears that wouldn't stop falling. "No, but I thank you for offering."

"Surely there must be something I can do. What has you so sad? You should be rejoicing about bringing a son home from Delphi."

She couldn't tell him what her true sorrow was. Very few knew about the child she'd borne Apollo. "I've learned he's my husband's child from some serving girl and he hasn't chosen to share the information with me." It angered her more than made her sad. Even though her father had married her to Xuthus as a reward for distinguishing himself in the war against the Euboeans and playing a significant role in defeating them, she'd thought he'd always respected her and had come to care for her over the years.

"How could he do that to you, mistress? To treat you like that is shameful. It isn't to be tolerated."

"I know we need an heir, but if only he'd told me. It's the deceit that upsets me the most." It didn't upset her nearly as much as Xuthus laying the blame on her for the lack of children in their union. She certainly wasn't barren.

"I'll do something about it, mistress. You shouldn't be forced to endure such an insult."

"No, nothing can be done. Didn't Apollo himself give us this child?" Thoughts of Apollo brought fresh tears.

"Weep no more, mistress. I'll take

care of everything for you. Surely you don't want some base born woman's child on the throne."

He was right, there was more than her feelings to consider. It was bad enough her husband was a foreigner, but to even think about putting some serving girl's son on the throne was an insult to all Athenians. "I have no idea what to do about the boy."

"I could slip poison into his wine cup during the adoption celebration tonight."

She didn't know what to do. Was a serving girl's son better than no heir at all? Why had she stopped to listen to Xuthus' conversation? Although she would have heard about it sooner or later as the man her husband had shared his secret with was one of the biggest gossips imaginable. Within days the entire town would know how he'd slighted her. By the end of the week it wouldn't surprise her if the entire country knew.

"Concern yourself with the problem no more. I'll take care of everything."

Before Creusa could protest, the elderly servant hurried off. She sighed heavily, wishing she'd never said anything to him. Again she thought of the beautiful baby she'd placed in the wicker basket and walked away from. Over the years she'd tried to console herself by believing his father would have looked after him and protected him and one day she'd have another child to help reduce some of the sorrow she felt over losing her firstborn. The second had never happened and now she was beginning to fear the first hadn't either. How was she going to bear it? This time she didn't bother wiping away the tears. There was no one to see them fall.

# Chapter Four: Ion

Dressing in his new finery, Ion wished he was back at the temple. He fingered the fine material of his garments, not wanting to attend the feast being thrown to celebrate his adoption. He wondered how his foster mother was doing and if she missed him. As soon as he was dressed, including new sandals on his feet, he made his way to the room that was packed with people awaiting his entrance. He felt like every eye in the room was upon him as he made his way to where Creusa and Xuthus sat. The older man beamed at him, an empty seat beside him. Ion guessed it was where he was meant to sit. His gaze was drawn to Creusa.

Unlike her husband, she didn't stare in his direction. Her gaze was firmly on the table in front of her and she looked sad. Was she regretting his arrival already? Or was something else going on? He had no idea who to believe in this place. Many had been friendly to him. Some had warned him against people he'd then seen them act friendly towards only minutes later. It made him wonder what they said behind his back. Sitting at the table, he thought of Apollo, and mentally besieged him for help. He wasn't certain what he needed help with the most. Surviving the meal or not running away from the path the god had chosen for him. It took all his willpower not to demand Apollo tell him why he'd brought him here. He sat beside Xuthus, dredging up an answering smile for the man.

Xuthus continued to smile broadly. "Welcome, my son. Today you truly become my son, given to me by Apollo." Xuthus rose to his feet and, still beaming, addressed those gathered.

Ion tried to concentrate, but his mind wandered as Xuthus continued to talk about the journey to Delphi and how grateful he was to Apollo for providing him with such a fine youth for his son. Looking around the room, he noticed he wasn't the only one who was bored. Some were talking amongst themselves and one even looked like he might fall asleep.

Many were attentive, some nodding, others smiling and a few were scowling. Were those the ones he needed to be careful around?

Reaching the end of his speech, Xuthus gestured servants forward to serve wine. An elderly servant stepped in front of another servant so he could be the one to fill Ion's cup. He took the cup the servant handed him and remembering his foster mother telling him not to forsake the gods, tipped a little onto the floor. He thanked Apollo for his blessings. Raising the cup to his mouth, he didn't get the chance to drink before a dove flew into the room and headed straight towards his face. He placed the cup on the table, rising to his feet to chase the bird away. He nearly stumbled over the elderly servant who'd remained beside his seat.

Instead of attacking him, like he'd expected, the dove landed on the table and drank from his cup. The bird began to quiver and shake, falling dead in front of him. Ion stared at the lifeless body, his attention drawn by a sound behind him. Turning, he saw it was the elderly servant backing away, his gaze fixed on the dove.

Anger race through Ion and he grabbed a knife from the table. He hadn't even wanted to be here. There was no need for anyone to try and kill him. If they'd asked, he would have left. "What have I done to you that you've tried to kill me?" Ignoring the exclamations of shock around him, he grabbed the elderly man by his tunic so he couldn't retreat further.

The man trembled, stumbling over

his words. He tried to pull away from Ion's grip.

Ion refused to let him escape, shaking the man. "Tell me."

The elderly man glanced towards Creusa. "I wanted to make my mistress happy."

Xuthus, who'd risen to his feet at the same time as Ion, stared at his wife. "You would kill our son? How could you destroy what Apollo has given us?"

Creusa rose to her feet, violently shaking her head. "No. I didn't ask this of him." Her gaze was drawn to the servant.

"I told you what I'd do to help and you didn't tell me no." The old man continued to look at Creusa.

Letting go of the old man, Ion took a step towards Creusa, the knife still grasped in his hand. "You wanted me dead?"

Creusa shook her head, taking a step away from him. Further retreat was prevented when she ran into her husband. She opened her mouth to speak, but was interrupted.

"Apollo came to me with a message."

Hearing the familiar voice, Ion's anger lessened slightly and he looked towards his foster mother, unable to believe she was standing in front of the table. When had she arrived? He heard the murmurs that went through the room. "The Oracle," some of them said, "The Pythia," others murmured. All of them stared at the woman standing in front of him, just like he did. She wore a crown of bay leaves and held a sprig of bay in one hand, a sack on the floor at her feet.

"You can't take our son away, not after giving him to us only days ago," Xuthus said.

Hope rose inside Ion. Was that it? Had she come to take him home? He obviously wasn't wanted here, regardless of how welcoming Xuthus had been. He was only one man. It would take more than the welcome of a single person to make him feel like he belonged.

"I've come to prevent a grave mistake."

What mistake? Ion couldn't think what mistake she was talking about. She was too late to have stopped them from poisoning him. His gaze was drawn to the dove lying on the table. He would have to go to Apollo's temple and make offerings to the god for saving him from that fate. What was the mistake his foster mother had come to prevent? Did they have more than one plan to end his life in case poisoning him failed?

"Apollo isn't taking my son from me?" Xuthus asked. "I had no knowledge of what this servant planned to do. You can't take Ion because of the actions of someone else."

"I would not take the child from his mother."

Ion could hear the speculation running through the room. The word mother was repeated numerous times. Was this his foster mother's way of saying she was taking him home? He wanted to beg her to take him with her.

"Who is his mother?" Creusa asked.

The Oracle stared directly at Creusa. "You are." When noise rose in the room behind her, the Oracle raised a hand and silence fell. "This is the child you gave birth to. Apollo's son."

Ion shook his head. It couldn't be possible. This woman was his mother? The woman who'd tried to kill him with the help of her servant.

"You had a child and told no one?" Xuthus demanded.

Creusa continued to stare at the Oracle. "Impossible."

"Are you denying your child? Are you telling all here that you never gave birth to Apollo's son?"

Creusa shook her head, looking half dazed. "I bore Apollo's child, but how could he still be alive? I beseeched Apollo to take care of him and protect him and tell me he still lived. I heard nothing. Not one little whisper that my baby survived."

"You deserted me? You left me on

the steps of the Delphi Temple and never thought to check on me again?" Ion stared at the woman who was supposedly his mother.

Creusa continued to shake her head. "No I put you in a wicker basket and hid you in a cave. I tried not to, but couldn't resist checking on you a couple of days after I'd left you there. You were gone. No sign that you'd ever existed, the ache in my heart my only reminder of you."

"Apollo asked Hermes to lift the basket and carry it to his temple for me to find," the Oracle said.

"Impossible." Creusa spoke softly, the words little more than a whisper.

"So you keep saying, and yet here he stands beside you, nearly killed by the hand of your trusted servant." The Oracle gestured towards Ion. "Are you going to continue to deny his existence?"

It was Ion that shook his head this time. Creusa couldn't possibly be his mother. "How could you desert me?"

Creusa turned towards him. "It's impossible. You can't be that baby. You can't imagine how many years I've mourned the life of that child. Leaving him in the cave was the only way I could think to give him a chance to survive. My father would never have believed the baby was Apollo's and would have had me and the infant killed."

The Oracle held up her hand. Charms dangled from worn cords. "Do you recognise these?" She took several steps forward, stopping at the edge of the table, the sack now held in the hand with the sprig of bay.

Creusa's hands covered her mouth. "It can't be."

"Are you saying this isn't enough proof?" Lowering her hand, the Oracle held out the sack. No one stepped forward to take it.

Taking pity on his foster mother, Ion placed the knife on the table and reached for the sack, removing a wicker basket from it. He stared at the aged item, placing it on a clear spot of the table.

Creusa burst into tears. "My son? He's truly my son?"

"The youth isn't my offspring?" Xuthus asked. No one paid him any attention.

The Oracle laid the charms on the table, her gaze still on Creusa. "This is the son you bore Apollo. He left him in my care. I didn't know until last night exactly who he is. Apollo told me to save him. He has ever protected his son."

"Thank you for returning him to me." Tears streamed down Creusa's face.

Ion felt odd. Apollo was his father? His mother hadn't abandoned him, but had been trying to protect him? After a lifetime of thinking he'd been deserted it was hard to believe. But it must be the truth. The Oracle never lied.

Creusa reached for his hands, clasping them tightly. "You can't believe how often I've dreamt of this moment."

"When I was younger I used to think that one day you'd turn up for me."

"You had a good childhood? I prayed that you did."

He nodded and glanced towards

his foster mother. "Yes. I might have wondered about you occasionally and wished to meet you and ask you why you'd left me on the temple steps, but I couldn't have asked for a better childhood. Or a better mother than my foster mother." He saw the pain his words caused Creusa, but he wasn't about to reject his foster mother after all she'd been to him.

"I'm glad." Still holding his hands, Creusa looked towards the Oracle. "Thank you."

"Why did you tell me I should regard the first person I met upon leaving the sanctuary, my son?" Xuthus asked.

"Apollo addressed both of you. As your wife's son, he is also your son. Are you not pleased to have a son after so many years without one?" the Oracle asked.

"Yes, of course. I'm sure he'll be a great comfort to me in my old age. When you said you wouldn't take Ion from his mother, you were telling us you were leaving him here?" Xuthus asked.

The Oracle smiled. "Not only will you have Ion, but eventually the two of you will bear a son you'll name Dorus. Your two sons will father great nations. Ion will father the Ionians and Dorus will father the Dorians."

Ion wanted to protest that he wasn't important enough to father great nations, but he knew the Oracle was never wrong. Instead, his gaze was drawn to the bird lying on the table near his cup and he sent thanks to Apollo for all he'd given him. Tomorrow he'd visit his father's temple and leave offerings to show

how much he appreciated everything he'd done for him.

His gaze was drawn to his foster mother who smiled fondly at him, a tinge of sadness in her expression. Next he looked towards Creusa who continued to hold his hands, tears streaming down her smiling face. Behind her stood Xuthus, his hand resting on his wife's shoulder with a grin that hadn't left his face since hearing what the future held.

Ion's lips slowly curved into a smile as his gaze returned to Creusa, his mother. Her hands tightened on his. He had no idea how he'd find an offering great enough to thank Apollo. It would take years of offerings and even that wouldn't be enough. Again he looked towards his foster mother. Nations? He wanted to ask her if she was certain, but she always was. Letting go of one of Creusa's hands, he straightened his shoulders. Somehow he'd prove he was worthy of fathering nations.

"I knew from the moment I first saw you in your wicker basket that you were someone special." The Oracle started to turn away, a sad smile on her face. "Maybe one day you'll return to Delphi to consult the Oracle."

Ion nodded and watched as her smile momentarily widened before she turned and walked towards the doorway. He'd make certain of it.

# Free Ebook

Subscribe to Avril's newsletter to receive a free ebook. This ebook is exclusive to those on her mailing list. To find out more about this offer visit: www.avrilsabine.com/free-ebook/

*

We value your privacy and will not sell, rent, exchange or loan your email address to third parties. Your information is confidential and you

are under no obligation to remain on
the mailing list and can unsubscribe at
any time.

# To The Reader

If you enjoyed this book, why not consider leaving a review to help other readers discover it too? Reader engagement is one of the few ways that lets an author know readers want more books in a particular series or genre. So leave a review and tell friends, not only about this book but also about other ones you've enjoyed, so you can continue to enjoy books by your favourite authors for years to come.

Dreams are meant to be lived,
Avril.

# About The Author

Avril is an Australian author who lives with her family on acreage in South East Queensland. She writes mostly young adult speculative fiction, but has been known to dabble in other genres. You can find more information about her at her website www.avrilsabine.com where you can also subscribe to her newsletter to be kept informed about new releases, current projects, blog posts and exclusive news.

# Titles By Avril Sabine

Stories about strong characters and characters who discover their strengths.

**SERIES**

*Assassins Of The Dead- Young Adult Fantasy/Paranormal*

Book 1: Dark Blade

Book 2: Dragon Touched

Book 3: Society Against Vampires

Book 4: King's Request

***Dragon Blood- Young Adult Urban Fantasy (with elements of romance)***

(5 book series)

Book 1: Pliethin

Book 2: Wyvern

Book 3: Surety

Book 4: Knight

Book 5: Mage

***Dragon Mage- Young Adult Urban Fantasy (with elements of romance)***

(Series two of Dragon Blood series)

Book 1: Promise

*Dragon Blood Chronicles- Young Adult Urban Fantasy (with elements of romance)*

(Companion stand alone series to Dragon Blood)

Book 1: Oath

Book 2: Betrayed

*Guardians Of The Round Table- Young Adult Fantasy LitRPG*

(Co-written with Storm and Rhys Petersen)

Book 1: Dexterity Fail

Book 2: Goblin Boots

Book 3: Singed Feathers

Book 4: Frog Mage

Book 5: Crystal Mine

Book 6: Cursed Harp

Book 7: Treasure Seeker


***Rosie's Rangers- Young Adult Western Steampunk***

(6 book series)

Book 1: Justice

Book 2: Vengeance

Book 3: Treachery

Book 4: Accused

Book 5: Wanted

Book 6: Corruption


*Mark Of Kings- Children's Fantasy*

(Upper middle grade/preteen)

(4 book series)

Book 1: The Arena

Book 2: The Island

Book 3: The Assassin

Book 4: The King

# STAND ALONE SERIES

*Demon Hunters- Young Adult Urban Fantasy/Horror (with elements of romance)*

Book 1: Blood Sacrifice

Book 2: Retribution

Book 3: Tainted

Book 4: Premonition

Book 5: Cursed

Book 6: Feud

Book 7: Extrication

*Plea Of The Damned- Young Adult Urban Fantasy/Paranormal*

(6 book series)

Book 1: Forgive Me Lucy

Book 2: Forgive Me Aiden

Book 3: Forgive Me Jena

Book 4: Forgive Me Kobe

Book 5: Forgive Me Marti

Book 6: Forgive Me Dawson

*Realms Of The Fae- Young Adult Urban Fantasy (with elements of romance)*

The Sword (short story in Like A Girl Anthology)

Heart Of Stone

Book 1: A Debt Owed

Book 2: Marked By The Hunt

Book 3: The Magic Collector

Book 4: An Unexpected Betrayal

Book 5: Imprisoned By Iron

*Fairytales Retold (Short Stories)*

Snow-White And Rose-Red

The Twelve Brothers

The Light Princess

Beauty And The Beast

Sleeping Beauty

Aschenputtel

The Golden Bird

The Frog Prince

The Death Of Koshchei The Deathless


*Myths And Legends Retold (Short Stories)*

Ion, Son Of Apollo

Sir Gawain And The Maid With The Narrow Sleeves

Princess Ilse, The Giant's Daughter

## YOUNG ADULT NOVELS

*Young Adult Fantasy (with elements of romance)*

Elf Sight

Earth Bound

*Young Adult Urban Fantasy*

Stone Warrior (with elements of romance)

The Jungle Inside

*Young Adult Contemporary (with elements of romance)*

Through Your Eyes

The Ugly Stepsister

Perfect Little Princess

*Young Adult Contemporary/ Paranormal*

Whispers In The Dark (with elements of romance and same sex relationships)

Over Too Soon (with elements of romance)

## *Young Adult Sci-Fi*

Experiment X-One-Six (Urban Sci-Fi/Superheroes)

An Endless Dawn (Post Apocalyptic Sci-Fi)


## CHILDREN'S BOOKS

Dragon Lord (Preteen/early teens) (Fantasy)

The Irish Wizard (Upper middle grade) (Urban Fantasy)

## SHORT STORIES

### *Urban Fantasy*

Eternally Late

Dealings With Joe

Glimpses (short story in That Moment When Anthology)

### *Contemporary*

The Brat Next Door

### *Fantasy LitRPG*

(Set in the same world as Guardians Of The Round Table Series)

Tales Of Inadon 1: The Disc (Co-written with Storm and Rhys Petersen) (short story in Game On! Anthology)

## *Post Apocalyptic Sci-Fi*

Compulsive Directive

## NONFICTION

A Year Of Weekly Writing Exercises (Creative Writing)

Cooking For Families With Allergies (Cooking) (Co-written with Storm Petersen)

Tell Me A Story, Grandma (Memoir)

*For the most up to date details on available titles visit:*

www.avrilsabine.com/books/
bibliography

# Disclaimer

This is a work of fiction. Names, characters, businesses, places, events and incidents are either the products of the author's imagination or used in a fictitious manner. Any resemblance to actual persons, living or dead, or actual events is purely coincidental. The opinions expressed or beliefs held are those of the characters and should not be assumed to be the opinions or beliefs of the author.